For Keelia, Blaine, and Eliot, and in loving memory of their shining Max —DH
For Sung-Sau So —MS

Text copyright © 2020 by Deborah Hopkinson.
Illustrations copyright © 2020 by Meilo So.

Library of Congress Cataloging-in-Publication Data:

Names: Hopkinson, Deborah, author. | So, Meilo, illustrator. Title: Butterflies belong here / by Deborah Hopkinson ; illustrated by Meilo So. Description: San Francisco : Chronicle Books LLC, [2020] | Summary: An immigrant girl explains how she learned English by reading about Monarch butterflies, and how, troubled by their decline, she got her classmates and neighbors together to build a butterfly garden. | Includes bibliographical references. Identifiers: LCCN 2018046397 | ISBN 9781452176802 (alk. paper) Subjects: LCSH: Monarch butterfly—Juvenile fiction. | Butterfly gardening—Juvenile fiction. | Immigrant children—Juvenile fiction. | Self-confidence—Juvenile fiction. | CYAC: Monarch butterfly—Fiction. | Butterfly gardens—Fiction. | Butterflies—Fiction. | Immigrants—Fiction. | Self-confidence—Fiction. | LCGFT: Picture books. Classification: LCC PZ7.H778125 Bu 2020 | DDC 813.54 [E] —dc23 LC record available at https://lccn.loc.gov/2018046397

Manufactured in China.

FSC
www.fsc.org
MIX
Paper from
responsible sources
FSC™ C008047

Design by Alice Seiler and Jill Turney.
Typeset in Harriet, Bizzle-Chizzle, Gill Sans, and Meilo font.

10 9 8 7 6 5 4 3 2 1

Chronicle Books LLC
680 Second Street
San Francisco, California 94107

Chronicle Books—we see things differently. Become part of our community at www.chroniclekids.com.

Butterflies Belong Here

A Story of One Idea, Thirty Kids, and a World of Butterflies

By Deborah Hopkinson

Illustrated by Meilo So

chronicle books · san francisco

SPRING

Last spring, we took a class picture.
That's me in the back.
I was a little like a caterpillar then:
quiet and almost invisible.
I didn't like to stand out or be noticed.

I know a lot about caterpillars and butterflies. That's because when I first came here, I couldn't read English. Our librarian helped me choose books with lots of pictures. My favorite had a butterfly on the cover.

Monarch butterflies are soft and gentle, like my baby brother. Some monarchs make a long, long journey, just like we did. They have to be strong to fly so far.

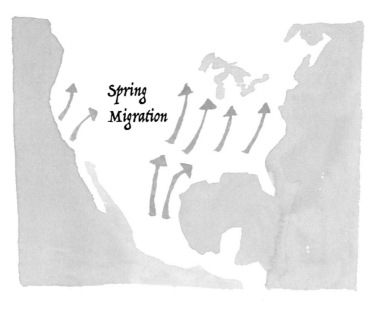

Spring
Migration

In March, monarchs head north from their overwintering
grounds. Most have spent the winter in Mexico during the
colder months, although some have stayed in Southern California.

The migrating females race against time, since they will only live a few
more weeks. They stop in the southern United States to lay their eggs, always
on one kind of plant: milkweed. This first generation born in the early spring
is the offspring of the monarchs who overwintered in Mexico. Each successive
generation travels farther north. It will take three to four generations to reach
the northern United States and Canada.

During the summer, non-migrating female butterflies only live three
to five weeks, but during that time they can lay hundreds of
eggs. They usually lay only one egg on each plant so each baby
caterpillar has enough food to eat.

After three to five days, a tiny caterpillar chews its way out of its egg. The caterpillar is the butterfly's larval stage.

It will be a caterpillar for ten to fourteen days. During this time, a caterpillar grows a lot, from 2–6 millimeters to 1–2 inches (25–45 millimeters).

A caterpillar is an invertebrate, which means it doesn't have a backbone like we do. As it grows, its soft, outer exoskeleton stretches until it can't stretch anymore, and then it splits. The caterpillar sheds, or molts, the old exoskeleton and grows a new one. This happens not just once, but five times.

SUMMER

When summer came,
I felt sure I'd see monarch butterflies.
I knew what to look for:
large black and orange wings
with a border of small white specks.

I wanted to see them
flit from flower to flower
sipping nectar.

But though I looked hard—
in parks, fields, and the community
gardens near our apartment—
I couldn't find even one.

I wondered if monarch butterflies
belonged here. Sometimes I
wondered if we did, too.

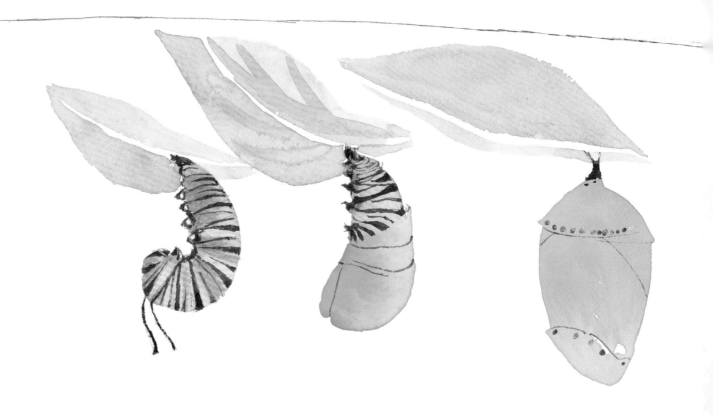

After a caterpillar has molted five times, it's ready to pupate. It looks for a safe spot. Then, if it's a butterfly caterpillar, it forms a chrysalis. If it's a moth caterpillar, it spins a cocoon.

Over the next eleven to fifteen days, the caterpillar transforms into an adult butterfly. Groups of cells in its body, called *imaginal discs*, develop into the parts of a butterfly: wings, organs, legs, and antennae.

The chrysalis darkens. Next comes *eclosure*, which means to emerge from the chrysalis as an adult butterfly.

The butterfly pushes its way out through a crack near the bottom.

Through a special process, the butterfly pumps fluid into its wings, which expand and take their final shape. It also presses the two parts of its proboscis together, which forms a straw that allows it to drink nectar.

Adult monarchs feed on nectar from many flowering plants such as coneflowers, butterfly bushes, sunflowers, verbena, and zinnias.

FALL

When school started again in the fall,
I ran to find the butterfly book
the very first time we visited the library.

It was easier for me to read it now,
and I found out why monarchs
have become so hard to find.

Monarchs need a special plant called milkweed. Female monarchs will lay their eggs only on milkweed. Not only that, when baby caterpillars break out of their eggs after three to five days, milkweed is *all* they eat. Milkweed and monarchs go together!

But butterflies have a hard time finding milkweed now. It used to grow wild in places where houses and cities now stand.

Some people think of milkweed as a useless weed, so they've used chemicals to keep it from growing in fields and on farmland. In other places, climate change has been causing droughts that make it difficult for milkweed to grow.

Milkweed is in trouble, and so monarchs are, too.
I learned that in 20 years, the number of
monarchs has fallen by 90 percent.

The problem is so big,
and butterflies are so small.

One day, our librarian called me over to her desk. "I know your class is working on research reports, so I bought a few new butterfly books. Maybe you'd like to be the first to check them out."

"Did you—did you get these just for me?" I asked.

"In a way." She laughed. "But lots of students like butterflies. I do, too. This summer I grew milkweed to make a monarch way station."

"I know what that is!" I said. "It's a special butterfly garden."

"That's right," she replied. "It needs at least ten plants, with two different kinds of milkweed, and nectar flowers for the butterflies to drink from."

I pointed out the window.
"That looks like a nice, sunny spot for a monarch way station."

She smiled. "It just takes one person to get things started."
And she looked at me.

"I'm not that kind of person," I whispered.

"Hmm," my librarian said.
"Did you know migrating monarchs fly
three thousand miles south to Mexico,
to spend the winter in a special place
they've never even been before?"

I *did* know that. "Butterflies are amazing!"

She nodded. "It's surprising what
such a tiny creature can do."

Four or five generations of monarchs are born in summer. Most adults live from two to six weeks, if they can escape being eaten by predators, such as birds or praying mantises.

The last generation of butterflies, born in early fall, is different. These butterflies will live seven or eight months—long enough to fly thousands of miles to the south to overwinter in Mexico and then turn north the following spring. Their wings may be larger and stronger. And they don't reproduce—not yet.

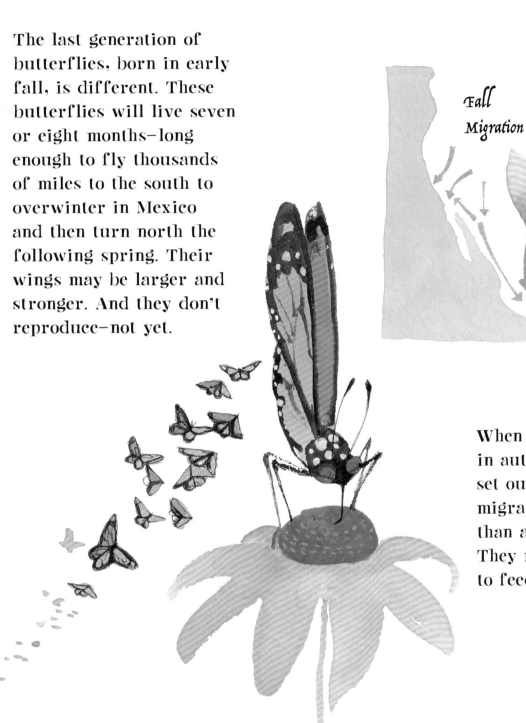

Fall Migration

When the days grow shorter in autumn, these monarchs set out on their amazing migration, flying farther than any other butterfly. They must stop many times to feed on the way.

WINTER

That winter, I imagined the butterflies,
high in the fir forests of Mexico,
waiting out the cold to make their long journey north.
I thought a lot about what it takes
to get things started.
I wondered if I'd ever be brave enough
to speak up, take charge,
and be noticed.

Monarch
Migration

It was hard for me to stand in front of class
and share my monarch research poster.
But my classmates loved my drawing of the
monarch's life cycle, my picture of
milkweed, and my migration map.

At the end, I told everyone, "We need
butterflies, and butterflies need us. All over
the country people are planting milkweed
and hoping to bring the monarchs back."

I was surprised by what happened next.
Questions flew here and there,
almost as if the room had filled with butterflies.
"Can we help the monarchs?"

"Do you know how to make a butterfly garden?"
"Could this be our new class project?"

★ WoW ★ Projects

Saving Sea
Turtles

Bees Are
the Best

Reduce Food
Waste:
Get a Chicken!

Monarch Migration

head north from
March
by planting
long their way
..l, monarchs

farther than any

"Slow down, everyone!" Our teacher
laughed, and turned to me.
"I'm hearing lots of interest in a
community action project.
Do you have ideas on how we could help?"

I could feel everyone's eyes on me.
I drew in a breath and turned my poster
around.

"This is my plan for a monarch way station,
the beginning of a timeline, a list of
supplies, and how much it might cost."

And that's how we got started.
The next weeks felt like a whirlwind.
I could feel myself growing and changing,
little by little.

We formed a team and talked to the principal about what we wanted to do.

Dear Parents,

Great news!!! We have got permission to build our own Monarch Way Station just outside the school library. There will be lots of fun events to raise money for the project, and we need your help with planting and fundraising! Donations of garden tools and gloves would be great, too!

Thank you,
from the Monarch Team

Monarch Fun Day Events

Butterfly Crafts
Plant Sale
Toy Swap
Freshly Pressed Juice Sale
Bake Sale
Music in the Park
Face Painting
Raffle

After that, we presented such a good plan to parents (they called it "solid and well thought-out") that they voted to give us money for supplies.

Fall: buy and plant baby milkweed plants

Winter: plants are dormant

Spring: plants grow but may not flower until second year

Milkweed Plants (the right kind of milkweed for our area)

To learn more about monarchs, we invited gardeners and scientists to class. We wrote letters to students in other places who are trying to help monarchs, too.

Our class made a presentation to the whole
school at assembly time.
Lots of other students signed up to help—
even kindergartners.

Our work took us outside school, too. We went to the town council to explain the importance of milkweed and ask that it not be poisoned. Instead, we showed why it should be planted in every city park. Afterward, the mayor shook my hand. "I hope you'll run for office someday. We need citizens like you."

Our friends and family helped build a fence,
design our garden, and find the best milkweed
for where we live.

Best of all was planting day.

While monarchs don't gather in a flock like birds before they set out, observers tend to see larger groups as the insects head south, especially when they roost at night. The butterflies stop to drink nectar along the way. A group of butterflies is called a swarm, a rabble, or a kaleidoscope.

In winter, monarchs west of the Rocky Mountains travel to small groves of trees on the California coast. The eastern population of North American monarchs spends the winter months, from October to mid-March, in about a dozen mountain areas in Mexico. Although the local people knew about the butterflies' overwintering sites, it wasn't until the 1970s that scientists found out about them.

During this time, the monarchs roost in the moist, cool canopy of trees called *oyamel* firs. The cool weather slows their metabolism. The moist air keeps them from drying out. They rely on their fat supplies rather than nectar.

In 2008, the Monarch Butterfly Biosphere Reserve in Mexico was named a World Heritage site. But monarchs continue to face challenges when trees in the forest are logged.

Usually, the butterflies head north in the second week of March. Will this be different with a changing climate? Scientists and ordinary people are working together to help find out. Citizen scientists tag butterflies and submit information on sightings to butterfly conservation organizations.

SPRING

Here's our new class picture. That's me in front, holding the sign.

Making the way station has been like a journey. And though we don't have monarchs yet, we got a chance to see butterflies when we visited students from another school who've already been helping monarchs for two years.

They told us how they serve as citizen scientists by raising caterpillars to become monarchs, carefully placing tags on their legs, then tracking their migration routes.

"Next year, we'll be monarch trackers, too," I said.

Meanwhile, my friends and I have lots to do. Even though school is out, summer will be busy. We'll take turns visiting our garden to weed and water. I'm in charge of reminding everyone. I can hardly wait to see our plants grow. And, of course, watch for butterflies.

Once, I tried to hide. But a caterpillar never stays the same for long. It grows and sheds its skin: one, two, three, four, five times before it forms a bright green chrysalis.

Then it emerges
as something new,
unexpected,
surprising.
Just like me.

AUTHOR'S NOTE

The characters in *Butterflies Belong Here* are made up. But the story is based on a real and serious issue: the decline of monarch butterflies.

Just like bees, butterflies and moths are pollinators. As these insects feed on nectar, they move pollen from one flower to another. This helps a plant make seeds for a new generation. Butterflies and caterpillars also provide food for other insects, birds, and animals.

I was inspired to write this story by reading about what children and communities all over our country are doing to help butterflies. I had another reason, too. As an author, I travel to schools across the country and meet students who have come from many different places. I often see children reaching out to newcomers to make them feel welcome and safe.

Young people all over are creating change and making our world better. Thank you!

Last year, I planted milkweed in my garden for the first time. I can't wait to plant more milkweed and flowering plants for monarchs. Together, let's bring the monarchs back!

Quick Guide to Making a Schoolyard Monarch Way Station

Please see the Internet Resources section for more information.

Create a Team
Involve teachers, staff members, students, and your principal. Invite maintenance staff, parents, and community members.

Do Your Research
Read books, look online, and reach out to local gardeners and scientists.

Select the RIGHT Milkweed
It's essential to plant milkweed native to your region of the country. And don't forget to include other flowers that bloom throughout the summer and fall so that adult butterflies have a diversity of nectar sources.

Choose a Site
Find a sunny spot for your new garden.

Make a To-Do List and Timeline
Include tasks such as sharing information with the community, getting school approval, making a budget, raising money, planting, watering, and maintenance.

Have Fun!
Get started. Don't forget to plan for times when school is closed. Who will water in the summer?

Involve Your Community
Invite a local radio or TV station to see your garden. Your work can inspire others.

Be a Citizen Scientist!
Some students are learning to raise monarchs and act as citizen scientists by tagging individual butterflies before releasing them. Tagging butterflies helps scientists learn even more.

Miscellaneous Monarch Facts

Animal kingdom: Animalia
Phylum: Arthropoda
Class: Insecta
Order: Lepidoptera
Family: Nymphalidae
Subfamily: Danainae
Genus: *Danaus*
Species: *plexippus*

Monarchs *(Danaus plexippus)* have six legs, though only four are easily seen. The other two legs, called brushfeet, are carried close to the body and help the insects find milkweed.

Since milkweed (genus: *Asclepias)* is essential to the monarchs' life cycle, these butterflies only venture as far north as it grows, which is near Winnipeg, Canada.

The last generation born in late summer or early fall is called the Methuselah Generation, after a man from the Bible said to have lived a long time. These butterflies live seven or eight months and mate the following spring.

Migrating monarchs travel about 3,000 miles from the United States and Canada to wintering grounds in Mexico. When the butterflies migrate to Mexico, they are going there for the first time. Yet, somehow, the monarchs are able to find the same spot as their ancestors.

Monarchs can't fly if their body temperature is too cold, usually about 55° Farenheit (13° Celsius) or cooler.

A Canadian scientist named Dr. Fred Urquhart (1911–2002) and his wife, Norah, spent years trying to discover where monarch butterflies spend the winter. In 1937, he began tagging butterflies and asked for help from citizens and other scientists to learn more about migration routes. Tagged butterflies had been found in Mexico but it wasn't until 1975, when local guides led Ken Brugger and Catalina Trail to an overwintering colony in the fir-forested mountains of central Mexico near Mexico City that the butterflies' Mexican overwintering grounds were widely known. There they discovered a butterfly that had been tagged in Minnesota. This confirmed the migratory nature of the Monarch. To learn more about the Monarch Watch Tagging Program, which was restarted in 1992, visit: https://monarchjointventure.org/images/uploads/presentations/lovett.pdf.

Asclepias is the Latin word for the milkweed genus, which contains dozens of different species. You can visit the Xerces Society to locate milkweed seeds and vendors for your state: http://xerces.org/milkweed-seed-finder/.

You can get information about milkweed from Monarch Watch or from a local nursery or a university extension service.

Books for Young Environmental Activists

Baumle, Kylee. *The Monarch: Saving our Most-Loved Butterfly*. Pittsburgh: St. Lynn's Press, 2017.

Pasternak, Carol. *How to Raise Monarch Butterflies: A Step-by-Step Guide for Kids*. Buffalo: Firefly Books, 2012.

Stewart, Melissa. Illustrated by Higgins Bond. *A Place for Butterflies*. Atlanta: Peachtree, 2006, 2014.

Books for Grown-Up Activists and Educators

Agrawal, Anurag. *Monarchs and Milkweed: A Migrating Butterfly, a Poisonous Plant, and their Remarkable Story of Coevolution*. Princeton: Princeton University Press, 2017.

Broda, Herbert W. *Schoolyard-Enhanced Learning: Using the Outdoors as an Instructional Tool, K-8*. Portland, ME: Stenhouse, 2007.

Danks, Sharon Gamson. *Asphalt to Ecosystems: Design Ideas for Schoolyard Transformation*. Oakland, CA: New Village Press, 2010.

Rea, Ba. *Learning from Monarchs: A Teachers' Handbook*. Union, WV: Bas Relief, 2010.

Internet Resources

Please note that websites often change.

Association of Fish and Wildlife Agencies: Teaching about the Magnificent Monarch
https://www.fishwildlife.org/application/files/4715/1630/6270/MonarchResourceGuide1217.pdf

Defenders of Wildlife
https://defenders.org/monarch-butterfly/basic-facts

Gardens with Wings
http://gardenswithwings.com/

Journey North
https://www.learner.org/jnorth/tm/symbolic/About.html

Million Pollinator Garden Challenge
http://millionpollinatorgardens.org/

Monarch Butterfly Biosphere Reserve
http://whc.unesco.org/en/list/1290

Monarch Gardens for Schools
https://www.stlouis-mo.gov/government/departments/planning/
sustainability/monarchs/upload/Final-Educator-Guide.pdf

Monarch Joint Venture
https://monarchjointventure.org/

North American Butterfly Association
http://www.naba.org/

University of Minnesota Monarch Lab
https://monarchlab.org/

USDA Forest Service: Monarch Butterfly Teacher and Student Resources
https://www.fs.fed.us/wildflowers/pollinators/Monarch_Butterfly/teacherandstudent/index.shtml

US Fish and Wildlife Service: Schoolyard Habitat Program
https://www.fws.gov/cno/conservation/Schoolyard.html